This edition published by Parragon Books Ltd
in November 2017 and distributed by

Parragon Inc.
440 Park Avenue South, 13th Floor
New York, NY 10016
www.parragon.com

Written by David Bedford
Illustrated by Brenna Vaughan and Henry St. Leger
Edited by Laura Baker
Designed by Ailsa Cullen

Production by Rob Simenton

ISBN 978-1-5270-0973-8

Printed in China

I love my Grandma

PaRragon

Bath • New York • Cologne • Melbourne • Delhi
Hong Kong • Shenzhen • Singapore

Little Hedgehog and Grandma Hedgehog
loved to play hide-and-seek together.
One day, when Grandma went to find
Little Hedgehog . . .

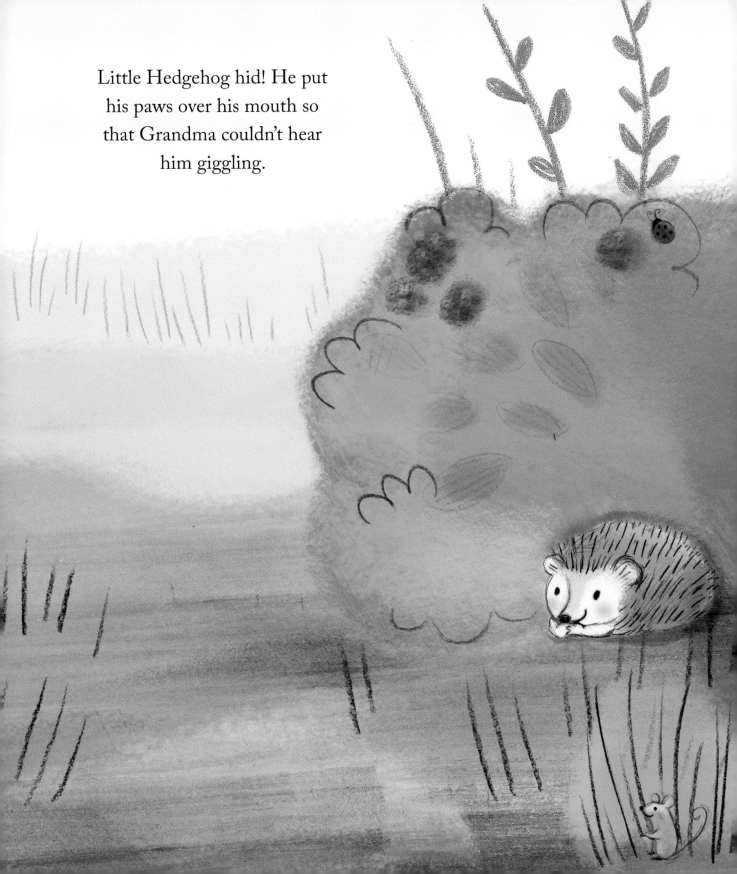

Little Hedgehog hid! He put
his paws over his mouth so
that Grandma couldn't hear
him giggling.

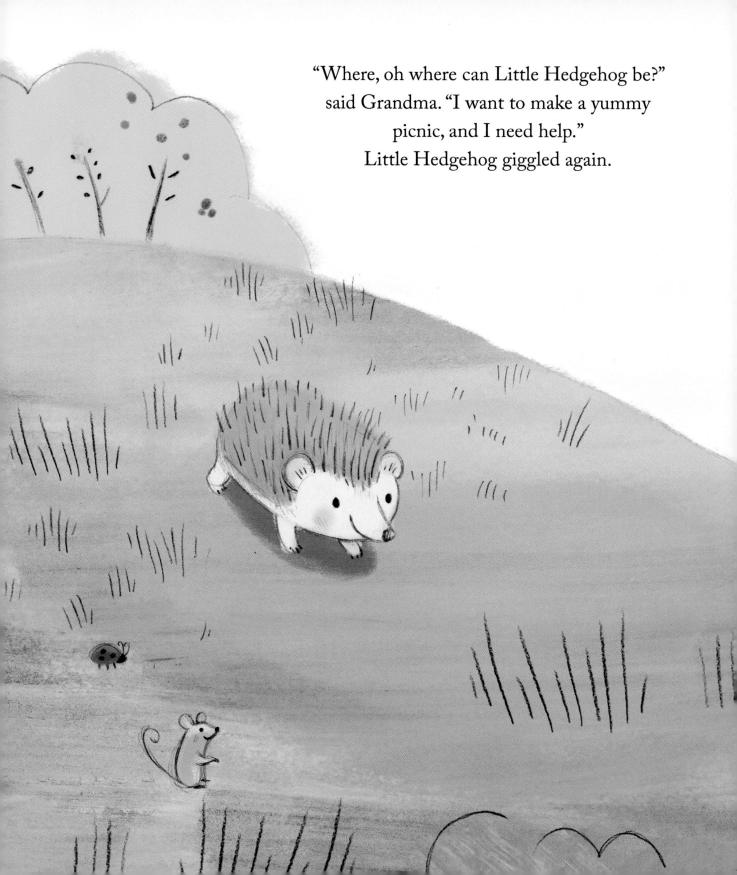

"Where, oh where can Little Hedgehog be?"
said Grandma. "I want to make a yummy
picnic, and I need help."
Little Hedgehog giggled again.

"Oh, well," said Grandma. "I will have
to make the picnic myself."
Little Hedgehog followed closely
behind Grandma.

"I wish Little Hedgehog were here to help me pick juicy blackberries," said Grandma.

When she wasn't looking, Little Hedgehog picked the **biggest blackberries** he could reach . . . and put them into Grandma's basket!

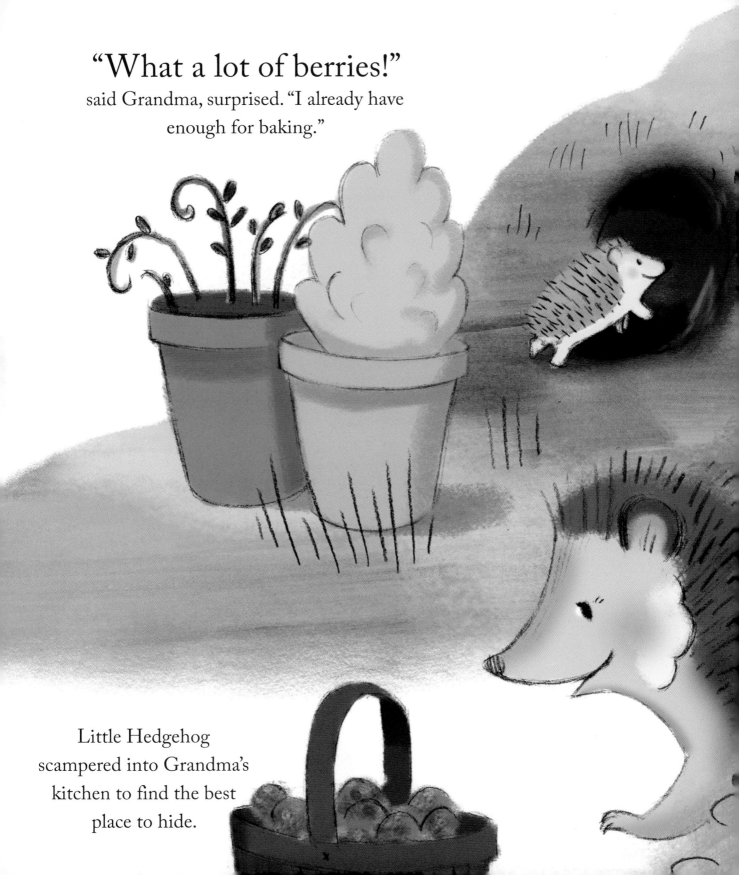

"What a lot of berries!"
said Grandma, surprised. "I already have
enough for baking."

Little Hedgehog
scampered into Grandma's
kitchen to find the best
place to hide.

Little Hedgehog crouched down low
so that Grandma couldn't see him.

"If only Little Hedgehog were here to help me!" said Grandma.

Little Hedgehog giggled again. Then he licked his lips as Grandma
Hedgehog poured sweet, scrumptious honey into her mixing bowl.

"Honey is my treat for Little Hedgehog," said Grandma.
Little Hedgehog crept out from his hiding place. . . .

He tried not to make a sound as he tasted the
honey for himself, but it was too good!

"Yum!"
whispered Little Hedgehog.

Then he hurried back to his hiding place. Suddenly . . .

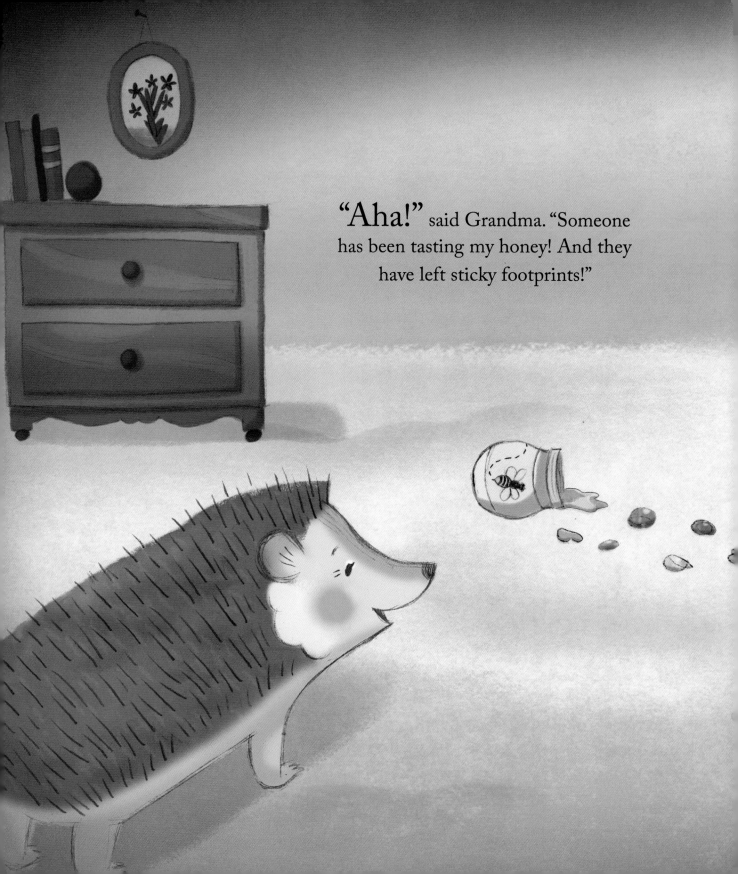

"Aha!" said Grandma. "Someone has been tasting my honey! And they have left sticky footprints!"

"Oh, no!" Little Hedgehog didn't want to be found. Not yet!

Grandma followed the
teeny,
tiny,
sticky
footprints
across the kitchen.

"Someone has been playing hide-and-seek
with me!" she said, smiling. Then . . .

"I've found you, Little Hedgehog!" said Grandma.

But Little Hedgehog wasn't behind the rocking chair.

There were only more sticky footprints. . . .

Grandma followed the sticky footprints out of
the kitchen and into the yard.

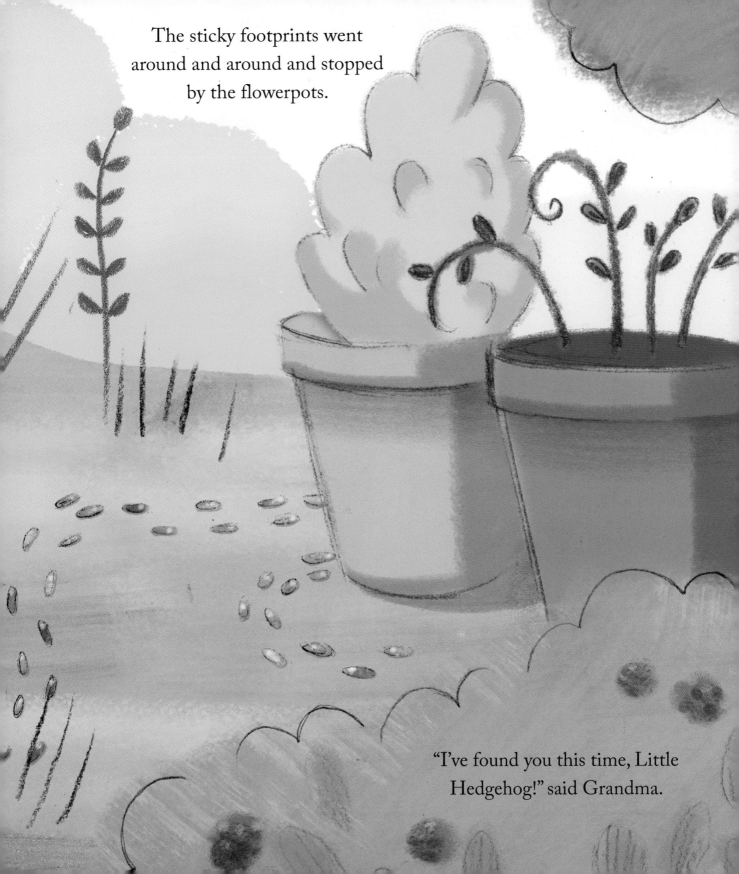

The sticky footprints went around and around and stopped by the flowerpots.

"I've found you this time, Little Hedgehog!" said Grandma.

But Little Hedgehog wasn't
behind the flowerpots!
He was . . . inside one!

"Surprise!"
said Little Hedgehog, giggling as
he gave Grandma a big hug.

"Wow, Little Hedgehog," said his grandma.
"You are the best at hide-and-seek. And I hope you are
hungry, because our picnic is ready!"

"I am hungry!" said Little Hedgehog. But when he looked around the yard, he couldn't see a picnic anywhere. "Where is it?" he asked. Grandma giggled.

"You have to find it!" she said.

Little Hedgehog searched
around the yard and
soon found . . .

honey cookies . . .

and fruit salad.

Then Grandma brought out a
giant blackberry and honey cake.

"Yum!"
said Little Hedgehog.
It was the best he had ever tasted.

"I love Grandma's picnics!"
Little Hedgehog shouted happily. "And . . .

"I love my grandma!"